WEiRDO

All rights reserved. Published by Scholastic Inc., *Publishers since 1920.* SCHOLASTIC and associated logos are trademarks and/or registered trademarks of Scholastic Inc.

The publisher does not have any control over and does not assume any responsibility for author or third-party websites or their content.

No part of this publication may be reproduced, stored in a retrieval system, or transmitted in any form or by any means, electronic, mechanical, photocopying, recording, or otherwise, without written permission of the publisher. For information regarding text permission, write to Scholastic Inc., Attention: Permissions Department, 557 Broadway, New York, NY 10012. For information regarding art permission, write to Scholastic Australia, an imprint of Scholastic Australia Pty Limited, 345 Pacific Highway, Lindfield NSW 2070 Australia.

ISBN 978-1-338-30558-6

10 9 8 7 6   19 20 21 22 23

Printed in the U.S.A. 23
This edition second printing 2019

Typeset in Grenadine MVB, Push Ups, and Lunch Box

BLAH.
BLAH.
BLAH

ANH DO

Illustrated by JULES FABER

WEiRDO

SCHOLASTIC INC.

CHAPTER 1

Here we go again. Even in a **new school**, in a **new town**, my year is about to start the **exact** same way it always does . . .

WHAT'S YOUR NAME?

WEIR.

"That's an interesting name. What's your last name?" says Miss Franklin.

That's the bit I **really** hate. Why does **everyone** have to ask for your **last name**?

"Weir, what's your last name?" she asks again.

DO.

DO? RHYMES WITH "GO"?

UH-HUH . . .

"Your name's . . . Weir *Do*? It's not really, is it?"

"Yes, actually, it is," I reply.

WEIRDO?

Get ready for it. In exactly **three** seconds, all the kids will start laughing . . .

ONE,
TWO,
THR—

HAHAHAHA!

That's the story of my life!

SO WHAT'S YOUR SISTER'S NAME? PLAY?

→ PLAY DO!

HA HA HA

WHAT'S YOUR FATHER'S NAME? TAE KWON?

↘ TAE KWON DO!

HA HA HA

What I would give for a last name like **Smith** or **Jones** or **Chapman** or **Fletcher**. Anything! Even **GoopGoop** goes better with Weir than Do.

What's your name?

Weir GOOPGOOP!

YAY!

I guess when they gave out last names,

I lost . . . big time.

Here we go, Weir . . .

Let's see what your last name will be . . .

Thing is, my dad was born in Vietnam. His last name is **Do**. (Yep, rhymes with "go.")

My mom's last name before she married my dad was **Weir**. She really loved that name, so I got lumped with Weir Do! **WEIRDO!**

My parents could have given me any first name at all, like **John, Kevin, Shmevin,**

ANYTHING!

What about Rusty? **Rusty Do** sounds like a movie star.

I'd like to thank my parents for my cool name!

Or maybe a famous country music singer.

I'm glad I'm not a Weirdooooooooooooo

Instead, I'm stuck with the **worst** name since **Mrs. Face** called her son **Butt**.

Now that was a **funny** roll call:

☑ **Kevin Clark**
☑ **Mary Connors**
☐ **Butt Face**

HAHA HA HA

Anyway, back to class . . .

"Children, it's **rude** to laugh at someone's name," says the teacher. "I'm sorry, Weir . . . *Do*. Please sit down, Weir . . . DO."

    And then it started.

I could tell the teacher was trying **really hard** not to laugh. It's a sign when people's cheeks puff up like they're about to **explode**.

I'm actually an expert on the subject.
I've seen it **a lot**.

My kindergarten teacher

My first-grade teacher

My second-grade teacher

The day I was born . . .

WHAT'S HIS NAME?

Granddad

Great Aunty Flo

Uncle Kenny

Cousin Fran

nurse

Aunty Jan

Dad with a 'stache

Young Sally

Finally, my new teacher ran out of the classroom . . .

BWA HA HAHA HAHAHA HA HAHA!

then she returned.

PLEASE
TAKE A SEAT,
WEIR . . .

I was so busy trying not to look embarrassed, I
forgot I was wearing my sister's old shoes . . .

and tripped.

16

That's when a **girl** reached down

to help me up.

As I looked into her face, I thought she was the

most beautiful ♡❤

girl in the world.

Her pencil case read

Bella Allen.

guess I should tell you a bit about my family.

My sister's name is Sally.

Why did *she* get the normal name? Not that **I'd** like to be called **Sally**.

Sally Do

Me

Sally is older than me by three years and she is one of those people who always saves up her Easter eggs for months and months. It used to be great finding her **hidden** pile of eggs in **June!**

But last year, she'd had enough of me eating her stash, so she invented a way to make sure I **never** touched them again.

Sally also likes to bug me with some **really** annoying habits.

DON'T COPY ME. → DON'T COPY ME.

GO AWAY. → GO AWAY.

ARGHHHH! → ARGHHHH!

Then Dad gave me some tips on how to get her back.

But then she figured out a way around it.

Sally's also one of those people who

always makes her bed...

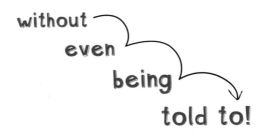

without

even

being

told to!

Sally's bed

My bed

In fact, almost **everything** she does makes me look

Sally's wardrobe

My wardrobe

Sally's homework

My homework

My little brother's name is **Roger**.

Another normal name, but read on ⟫⟫

he's **NOT** normal.

Roger (not
    normal)

He has just become tall enough to use the toilet
instead of his potty. But it's not going so well
so far. For the **third time** this week, he's
slammed the toilet seat on his **thing** . . .

He's also been dipping stuff in his baby food.
Often **stuff that is important.**

PHONE WANT
EAT PUDDING?

Roger is just starting to talk, and some words come out **funny**. Like when he tries to say **Father**, it sounds more like something else.

SAY
"FATHER."

SAY "**BIG** FATHER!"

BIG FARTER!

BIG FARTER! BIG FARTER!

Big Farter is actually a good way to describe Dad.

My dad is one of those dads who tells you not to **pass gas** in public, but then when he feels like it, he just goes ahead and **FARTS**.

RRRRRIIPPP!!!

If Mom's nearby, Dad will try to blame it on something else that **couldn't possibly** have made such a **big** noise.

Like . . .

But if Mom's not around and it's just us kids,
Dad likes to **boast**.

And here's a tip, if my dad ever asks you to pull his finger . . .

DON'T!

Just run the other way!

PULL MY
FINGER . . .

If you're **too slow**, it's time to get out the **clothespins**.

Here's my mom. She's one of those people who **loves** to save money. I don't want to call her **cheap** ... but she is.

She won't even let me change the water after Roger has a bath. And if Roger's been playing in the **dirt** all day, I think I come out **dirtier** than when I went in.

But **the worst** thing she does is she **licks** her hand to **fix up my hair**.

WEIR. COME HERE. YOU'VE GOT A HAIR OUT OF PLACE.

SLURP!

Great. Now I look like the **world's biggest nerd** and **smell** like the **tuna sandwich** Mom had at lunch.

Mom's cheapness also explains why I was wearing **my sister's shoes** on the first day of school.

They don't really fit yet, but Mom says they will encourage my feet to grow.

As if shoes
    speak to feet!

CMON, FEETY FEETY, YOU NEED TO GROW NOW.

NUH.

The **craziest** person in our family is **Granddad**.
He is Mom's dad and he is

         really, really, really old.

He is so old, sometimes bits of him just fall
out.

WHAT'S THIS IN
MY SOUP?

OH. THAT'S WHERE MY
ROBOTIC EAR WENT!

But he always pops
everything back in place.

SQUELCH!

If I got to choose robotic parts, I'd get some **really fast legs**. I'm not a very fast runner. When they handed out **fast running**, I lost out.

I lost out on **tallness**, too.

And on **good hair**.

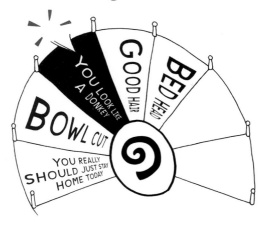

I'm a bit different, I won't lie. **WEIRDO's** not just my name. It kind of **describes the way I am . . .**

Like, whenever I eat a hamburger, the meat **always** falls out the bottom. I hate that.

And whenever I pull off a Band-Aid, I always **rip off my scab**, too.

I can't eat the **stringy** stuff on the inside of a banana. That stuff tastes **strange**.

But **I LIKE** lots of weird things, too, like when it's **hot** at night and you turn your pillow over, the other side is **nice and COOL!**

Like an **extra** pillow! **I love that!**

I also like it when you have to **PEE REALLY BADLY** and you find a toilet just in time.

AAAAAHH!

Or when there's an ad break on your **favorite** TV show, and you run out to do something really important, but then you come back **just in time!**

It's also great when you mix up a packet of **cheesy macaroni,** and halfway through eating it, you get that one

▸ bright orange macaroni bit

with

stacks of flavor

stuck on it!

YAY!

But most of all, **I love to draw!**

I like drawing

anything,

anywhere.

I even like drawing on the steamy mirror after a bath.

What I like drawing the most are animals.
Not just any animals, but

WEIRD animals.

I like to mix them up!

My favorite is a **duck** crossed with a **poodle**:

Duck + Poodle
= DOODLE!

Or a **fish** crossed with a **cat**:

Fish + Cat
= FAT!

Or a **frog** crossed with a **pug**:

Frog + Pug
= FRUG!

At the end of the day, things aren't too bad.
There are some things that I'm **GOOD AT**.

Like **spelling** . . .

And **remembering people's names**.

I do this by making a picture in my mind of something that **rhymes** with a person's name.

Like I remembered the name of a girl from my old school called **Alana Stead** by thinking of the words

Banana Head.

Butt Face

Of course **Mrs. Face's** kid is **easy!**

CHAPTER 3

Let's get back to my first day in my new school.

The bell rang for outdoor lunch, and I followed everyone out into the playground.

I could see it was a normal playground with all the normal silliness.

HOW TO:
Smell the cheese

BOOYAH!

I can't believe some kids still fall for that!

HOW TO: Arm Burn

OUCH!

HOW TO: Wedgie

EEK!

HOW TO:
Shoe Lacing

WHOA!

I looked over to the corner and saw Bella Allen sitting with another girl from our class. It looked like she was about to get a

Wet Willy in her ear!

I rushed over to save her but **tripped** and **fell** again!

Stupid shoes!

So I called out from the ground . . .

BELLA!
WATCH OUT!

She turned and—

WET WILLY!

Oh **NO!** I just caused Bella to get a
poke in the eye.

I ran away and hid.

That afternoon we had our first gym lesson with **Mr. McDool**. His name is **easy** to remember.

Mr. McDool told us we were going to have our very own **class Olympics**. To make it seem more real, he even lit an old candle and called it the **Olympic torch**. He held it up high and some wax tipped out,

burning his armpit.

OUCH!

Mr. McDool made ribbons to give out for
first, second, and third in the running races.
I wish they had ribbons for **second last**.

I'm **really good**
at coming in **second last**.

I've learned to hang back in the running course. Don't line up along a bunch of guys who look fast. Line up near the end with the guys who look **slow**.

You can tell |slow guys| by a few surefire signs.

Socks pulled up too high.

Pants pulled up too high.

Finger always in nose.

Finger always in someone else's nose.

But usually the best way to tell who's the slowest is by finding the guy who's got the top bit of his **butt crack** showing. He's almost **always** going to be slow.

In my new class, that kid's name was **Toby Hogan**. The others were calling him **Piggy Bank** because it looked like his **butt crack** was a **coin slot**. He was the **perfect** choice to race with.

Well, someone must have put a

hundred dollars

in the coin slot before Toby's run, because
it turned out

Toby Hogan was

super fast! ⟫⟫

← Me! Second last again!

We were standing around waiting for a row of girls to race when a kid called Josh Keenan started showing off his arm muscles. Before I knew what was happening, it turned into a **muscle contest**.

Great, another contest for me to come in.

Or worse, last!

I tried to walk away, but it was too late. It would've looked like I was **chickening out**. Everyone's muscles were going to be bigger than mine.

So when it was my turn, I did the

<u>very best flex</u> I could manage.

Toby Hogan

YOUR MUSCLES ARE HUGE, WEIR!

WHOOO!

They didn't know I was doing
a trick that Dad showed me . . .

It was going so well that I started **showing off** and turning so that all the **girls** could see.

That's when Toby Hogan saw what I was doing and **busted** me.

HEY, THE NEW KID'S PUSHING UP HIS MUSCLE WITH HIS OTHER HAND!

CHEAT!

FIBBER!

Then they all started **shouting**:

LIAR, LIAR, PANTS ON FIRE!

I thought they were just saying it 'cause it rhymes, but it turns out they weren't. I'd backed into **Mr. McDool's Olympic torch** and

my pants **really** were

on fire!

Mr. McDool chucked a bucket of water on me to put it out.

There's that look again . . . he's trying not to laugh!

I stood there **dripping wet** while my whole class, including *Bella Allen*, stared at me like I was a complete . . .

weirdo.

The fire **burned a hole** right in the middle of my school shorts. For the rest of the day, I had to walk around sideways with my back to the wall so no one could see my **frog** undies.

I couldn't wait till the bell at the end of the first day. When Mom came to pick me up, I ran to her as fast as I could.

When I ran past Bella, she called out, **"Nice frogs!"**

UGH!

I went blank! Half my brain wanted to call back: **"Frogs are the best."** The other half wanted to say: **"Frogs are the coolest."** But it came out all wrong.

FROGS
ARE THE
BOOLEST!

ARGHHHHHH!

Boolest! Who says **Boolest???!!!**

What a way to start the new year!

CHAPTER 4

The next day at school, there was **awesome news.** Another new kid was starting. Since I had been there a **whole day already**, he was now the **new guy**.

And when he walked in, it got **even better**.

the ~new~ new guy!

I thought to myself, **YES!**

This guy makes me look
SUPER normal!

He's going to take some of the attention off me . . .

and I was right!

Henry quickly became the **strangest** guy in the class. He did everything a bit **differently**. Like when you said his name, it took three tries before he'd turn around.

HENRY!
HENRY!!
HENRY!!!

HUH?

And he has his own versions of nursery rhymes . . .

Mary had a little lamb,
Who one day just
dropped dead.
Now it goes to school
with her,
Between two chunks
of bread.

Well, the other kids think he's **strange**, but I think he's pretty **funny**.

That afternoon, I found myself standing in line outside the PRINCIPAL's office. Henry was there, too.

HI, HENRY.

HENRY!

HENRY!

HI, WEIR!

PRINCIPAL

76

Turns out we were both there because of one guy ⟶ **Blake Green**. It hadn't taken us long to figure out that just about everything that Blake Green tells you to do, **you shouldn't do**.

When Blake first saw Henry, he got the same look on his face that a dog gets when it looks at your ham sandwich.

dog

ham sandwich

Blake Green

Henry

Henry told me what Blake Green made him do. Henry was there because Blake tricked him into going into the **girls' bathroom**.

Here's what happened to **me**:

I managed to get **three** teachers angry
with **one** bread roll.

When it was my turn to go into the principal's office, Henry did something I **wasn't** expecting.

MR. HARRIS, WEIR DIDN'T MEAN TO THROW THE BREAD ROLL THROUGH THE WINDOW. HE TRIPPED IN HIS SISTER'S SHOES AND HIS LUNCH WENT FLYING OUT OF HIS HANDS.

He helped me out!

So I thought I ought to help him out, too.

HENRY WAS JUST LOOKING FOR HIS SCHOOLBAG. BLAKE TOLD HIM IT WAS IN THE BATHROOM. HE DIDN'T REALIZE IT WAS THE GIRLS' BATHROOM. HE'S NEW.

We **grinned** at each other, both convinced that we were

<u>out</u>

of trouble.

But when we walked in, I got the
best surprise of my life!

Bella was in detention, too! She was in
trouble for accidentally elbowing the girl who
gave her the **wet willy!**

Bella is easily the **prettiest** girl in the class.
Well, whenever Jenny, Clare, Mary, Sue, Yana,
and Wendy are away.

Bella!

Jenny Clare Mary Sue Yana Wendy

But I liked her. I liked her **a lot!**

And it turned out Henry liked her, too!

As soon as we walked in, he tried out one of his **super smooth**, **talking-to-girls** tricks:

HI. BELLA.
WANT TO HEAR
MY SPECIAL
NURSERY RHYME?

There was a little bunny, whose nose was very runny. If you think it's very funny, well, it's SNOT!

Bella moved away from Henry and closer to me. That's when I realized that with Henry as my sidekick, **I'd always be the cool one!**

cool one

So that's how me and Henry became

best friends.

or the rest of the week, me and Henry got up to **loads** of **funny business.**

I CAN MAKE YOU
FALL OVER WITH THE
POWER OF MY MIND.

Henry thinks my drawings are **cool**, so I've been making some **really funny** ones for him:

A

Frilled-neck | lizard

B Fold line B over
to meet line A

sausage dog

A

SKINK

A

CHAPTER 6

The school principal, Mr. Harris, came in to talk to our class about a **very important** matter.

"Kids, we've recently discovered that many of you have animals living in your hair called **lice**."

Animals living in my hair?! At first, I thought:

HOW COOL!

But it turns out, these things are not so good for you. They're tiny insects that **suck your blood** and make your head **itchy**.

RARR!

Mr. Harris then told us all to line up so some **lice inspectors** could check our heads.

I really hoped these guys didn't **check for worms** as well, because I wanted to keep my pants on.

They told us that if your head was **itchy**, it meant you probably had **lice**.

As soon as they said this, my head felt itchy, but I didn't want to scratch it. I think everyone felt the same. We all stood there with **itchy** heads that we were

too afraid to scratch!

At the end of it, Mr. Harris told us that **we all had lice.**

The **whole** class!

We were each given a bottle of shampoo and told to stay home **(yay!)** until we'd really washed our hair.

Then he told us that these **creatures** were brought to school by someone carrying them in their hair, and it all started a few days ago.

Well, **of course** everyone right away turned to Henry. He'd just turned up a few days ago, and he had this **guilty** look on his face.

It **must've** been him!

I'd just made a new friend, and now he was the **lice guy!** I'd have to stay away from him . . .

It felt like this one time Mom let me choose a Transformer for Christmas, then she wrapped it up and I couldn't have it for a month!

Suddenly, we heard some **chirping** noises in the classroom.

meep
meep

At first, I thought it was my **sister** hiding in the locker with the **hiccups**.

meep
meep

No one knew what the noise was. So Miss Franklin told us all to go around the classroom and look for the **mysterious** noise.

We looked for ages, but **found nothing.**

Then Henry put up his hand.

**MISS,
IT SOUNDS
LIKE BABY
SPARROWS.**

"How do you know that, Henry?"
said Miss Franklin.

"We had **lots** of birds on our farm, so I know
what they sound like."

"Do you know where they are?" the teacher asked.

"Sparrows like to nest up high," said Henry.
"I think they're **in the ceiling**."

Next, the school called some **bird inspectors** to come to our classroom and check the ceiling. And, sure enough, **Henry was right**.

There was a nest up there, and not only that, it was the sparrows who were responsible for everyone's lice.

They found **lots** of **bird lice** in the nest!

Henry became the

class hero for solving

The Mystery of the Chirping Noise

and everyone also realized that it wasn't him who gave us all lice.

All of a sudden I was **best friends** with the

coolest kid
in the class.

DON'T FORGET
I WAS HIS
FRIEND FIRST!

The very next day, Henry was back to being himself.

LOOK AT ME,
I'M A
WALRUS.

Oh well, at least I have him **all to myself again**.

CHAPTER 7

It was **show-and-tell** day, and I decided to take my **robotic ninja hamster** to school. He looked pretty dirty and needed a wash, so I turned on the sink faucet and heard a **huge scream!**

Sally

EEEEEEEEKK!

WHO TURNED ON THE TAP????

Sally was in the middle of a shower. Oops.
So when she came out, she got me back by
tying my school pants together.
When I went to put them on, I fell and
banged my head!

So I got her back by
putting glue in her shoes.

At school, Bella spent all of lunch handing out invitations to her **birthday party**.

Everyone in my class got an invitation.

Everyone except me.

When she was handing them out and she got to me, she smiled and then walked right past.

She even gave one to Toby Hogan. She must have liked what he brought in for show-and-tell.

THIS IS WHAT YOU CALL A PIGGY BANK.

Even **Henry** got an invitation!

Henry's toilet paper-dispensing helmet

WOOHOO!

What a bummer. She must have thought my **robotic ninja hamster** was weird. **Just like me.** Could this day get any **worse?**

After school, I heard Mom on the phone talking to Bella's mom! Then Mom gave me the **worst news I could ever hear.**

BELLA'S MOM HAS TO TAKE HER GRANDMA TO THE DOCTOR THIS AFTERNOON, SO BELLA IS COMING OVER TO OUR HOUSE. ISN'T THAT NICE?

NOOOOOOOO!!!!!

No one's been over to my house yet. Not even Henry. **My family is <u>too</u> weird!** But it was too late, and before I knew it,

Bella was at our front door.

"This is Weir's granddad, Bob," said my mom.

HELLO THERE. HOW ABOUT A HUG FOR AN OLD MAN?

OH NO, I've seen him do this before!

ARHHH!
YOU'VE
BROKEN
MY MOUTH!

"Sorry about that, Bella!" said my mom.

"Just kidding!" said Granddad. "They come out.
Look. Isn't that cool?"

Then Granddad put his teeth in backward and accidentally bit his tongue. He **screamed**.

AHHHHH!

Suddenly, there was another **loud scream**, coming from the bathroom.

OWWW!

UH-OH, IT SOUNDS LIKE ROGER'S SLAMMED THE TOILET SEAT ON HIS **THING** AGAIN.

I don't like making stuff up, but in this case, **I had to.**

HE LIKES TO CALL HIS HAND A "THING." LIKE RAHHHH, HAND THINGY.

My family is like one **disaster** waiting to happen after another!

Then my **worst fear** happened. Dad came home early from work. He walked right up to me and said the **baddest** thing he could say.

PULL MY FINGER!

DAD, NOOOOOO!!!

But it turns out he wasn't going
to **embarrass** me after all.

PLEASE, I'VE
GOT A CRAMP IN
MY HAND!

So Mom gave Dad a
quick hand massage.

Too many **close calls** so far, but overall, things were still all right.

Me and Bella were talking about the toys we'd brought in for show-and-tell. My **ninja hamster** was giving her **scientist doll** a ride on his back.

That's when Sally came out of her room.

Oh no, I forgot about the glue I put in her shoes!

She marched right up to where me and Bella were sitting.

SEE THOSE SHOES WEIR IS WEARING? THEY'RE ACTUALLY **MY OLD SCHOOL SHOES.**

NOOOOOOO!

My life is
destroyed!

But then Bella said something that I didn't expect at all!

HEY, THAT'S KINDA COOL. MY SCHOOLBAG USED TO BELONG TO MY BROTHER.

HUH?

WOW. This is **actually** going **great!**

I was just starting to feel really good about things when the doorbell rang . . . **What now?!**

I looked down the
hallway and saw
Henry at the door!

WHAT ARE YOU DOING, HENRY?

I'M WAITING FOR YOU TO LET ME IN!

"But why are you wearing
THAT?!" I asked him.

"Because I have a co—"

OOO!

Henry's **big green booger** hit me in the eye!

I turned and accidentally **knocked Bella over.** That's when the **booger** flew from my face onto Bella's!

YUCK!

I tried to wipe it off her with Henry's toilet paper.

And that's when I spotted **Roger running down the hall** with Bella's doll!

I **panicked** and couldn't think properly. I turned to Bella and probably said the **uncoolest** thing you could say to a girl.

UH, ME NEED GO PEE-PEE NOW!

I raced after Roger, but by the time I got to his room, it was **too late**.

DOLL EAT
PUDDING.

The doll's head was covered in **yellow goop!**

What do I do now?!?!

Sally and Henry raced in after me.

QUICK, GET
SOME WATER TO
WASH HER.

I ran back out to the kitchen, where Bella was sitting and filled up two cups of water. She looked at me **confused**.

UH, I LIKE TO DRINK TWO CUPS OF WATER BEFORE I GO TO THE TOILET . . .

IT HELPS ME GO PEE-PEE.

OKAAAAAY.

When I got back to Roger's room, there was pudding **everywhere!**

QUICK,
TO THE BATHROOM!

I grabbed the doll and ran to the bathroom. Sally and Henry followed.

Granddad was in there and we **squeezed** past him to get to the sink.

We were all hovering over the doll when Mom, Bella's mom, and Bella walked in to see what all the **fuss** was about.

Granddad tried to explain . . .

WE FOUND A COUPLE OF **LICE** ON BELLA'S DOLL. SO WE'VE JUST GIVEN HER A LITTLE HAIR WASH WITH THIS **LICE SHAMPOO**.

We cleaned up the doll just in time to hand her back to Bella.

OH, THANK YOU
FOR DOING THAT.

It was time to say bye to Bella, and I was
sure she thought I was **even weirder** than
before, thanks to my **crazy** family.

BYE, WEIR.
YOUR
FAMILY IS
REALLY
FUNNY!

Then she pulled an envelope out of her schoolbag.

I DIDN'T WANT TO GIVE THIS TO YOU IN FRONT OF EVERYONE AT SCHOOL.

It was an **invitation** to her birthday party that she'd drawn herself.

I LOVE **FROGS**, TOO. I THINK THEY'RE THE **BOOLEST**!

Invitation

A **special birthday invitation** from the **seventh-best-looking girl** at school.

This could be . . .

the **BEST** year ever!

MORE
TO COME!

For my three **favourite**

WeirDos!

FROM ANH

Xavier, Luc, and Leon

DEDICATIONS

FROM JULES

For all the kids with **nits**